HEATHCLIFF® HAS SPRING FEVER

by Laura Hitchcock

Illustrated by John Costanza

Watermill Press

Produced by Parachute Press, Inc.

©1990 Geo. Gately

What a beautiful spring day it was in West Finster!

"What shall we do today, pal?" Iggy asked Heathcliff.

Heathcliff didn't need to be asked twice. He gobbled his breakfast and raced for the back door—dragging Iggy right behind!

"Hey, wait till I finish eating!" cried Iggy.

Grandpa Nutmeg sighed. "Heathcliff, why can't you behave like other cats?"

But Heathcliff could never be an ordinary kitty—he's the roughest, toughest cat in West Finster! Left to himself, Heathcliff knows how to cause more trouble than a herd of stampeding elephants.

The people of West Finster have known that for a long time. But since it was such a nice day, Heathcliff decided to remind them once again!

Suddenly, something odd happened.

As Heathcliff tossed one last garbage can, a ray of sunlight hit him in the eyes.

Heathcliff stopped in his tracks, and a strange look came over him.

"**A**re you OK?"cried Iggy. "What's wrong?"

Heathcliff didn't answer for a moment. Then, he smiled slowly...and began cleaning up all the garbage cans he'd wrecked!

Iggy couldn't believe his eyes. Neither could the neighbors!

After he finished cleaning up the garbage, Heathcliff escorted Sonja all around the neighborhood.

Sonja purred. She loved having Heathcliff pay attention to her. If he behaved like a noble gentleman, so much the better!

At least, it was better at first. Sonja wasn't so happy when Heathcliff offered to escort Crazy Shirley, too!

"Hoo-boy!" said Iggy. "Now I know something's wrong! Heathcliff usually tries to run away from Crazy Shirley!"

All morning long, Heathcliff was polite and kind to everyone. By lunchtime, Iggy was worried.

"Heathcliff is acting so strangely," he told Grandma and Grandpa. "I think he might be sick!"

"I don't see anything wrong," replied Grandma. "In fact, I've never seen Heathcliff act this well before. He even wiped his feet before coming inside!"

"That's what I mean!" Iggy cried. Grandpa was going to agree with Grandma... but then he noticed Heathcliff was being polite and kind to the mice, too. He'd even spread a dinner for them.

"Time to visit the vet," Grandpa shouted. "NOW!"

The nurse asked Heathcliff, Iggy, and Grandpa to wait while the veterinarian prepared for their appointment.

After a long time, the vet finally came out—wearing a mask, thick gloves, and lots of protective clothing!

"Sorry to make you wait," he explained, "but it takes time to get ready for Heathcliff! That feisty kitty is always hard to handle."

But to the veterinarian's surprise, Heathcliff wasn't feeling feisty at all. He examined Heathcliff all over, from top to bottom... and for once, Heathcliff didn't mind a bit.

"This cat has a fever," the vet announced, at last. "Spring Fever!"

He explained that Spring Fever affects some cats in springtime. Any cat who gets it becomes sickeningly nice!

"The fever will stop when spring ends," he added. "Other than that, no one knows a cure!"

Back home, Iggy sat on the front steps and thought about Heathcliff's new personality.

"Guess I'll just have to watch out for you, pal!" he told Heathcliff. "At least until summer gets here."

Just then Muggsy and Spike showed up.

"Hey, Nutmeg !" called Muggsy. "You and your cat wanna play baseball? Heathcliff can be the baseball! Har-Har!"

Spike wanted to beat up Heathcliff, but Heathcliff didn't want to fight. Instead, he planted a big kiss on the end of Spike's nose!

"So your cat's turned into a sissy, eh, Nutmeg?" Muggsy sneered. "Guess he won't be able to help you out!"

"Don't bother Heathcliff!" said Iggy. "He's sick!"

Muggsy laughed, but he didn't bother Heathcliff. No—he tripped Iggy instead!

But when Heathcliff saw Iggy was in trouble, something strange came over him... again.

Suddenly, Heathcliff sprang into action! He sure didn't have Spring Fever now! Somehow, seeing Iggy in trouble had jolted him back into real life.

Iggy was happy to have his friend back to normal. And it didn't hurt that Heathcliff was tough enough to beat both Muggsy and Spike with one paw tied behind his back.

"Hurray for Heathcliff!" cried Iggy.

It didn't take long to get rid of Muggsy and Spike. Iggy barely saw them run off. He ran to Heathcliff, and threw both arms around his best friend.

"I'm glad you got over your Spring Fever!" Iggy said. "It doesn't really matter, though—I don't care if you're nice or naughty. For me, Heathcliff, you're always perfect!"